<u>New Expanded Edition</u>

TO TRAVEL LITE, PART 1.5

The Day Two Canines Informally Confessed

DENISE SHARP

Table of Contents

With so many lives ravaged, brokenhearted, livelihoods dismantled; and families feeling hopelessly overwhelmed not knowing what their tomorrow would resemble. As businesses of all sizes began scaling back and closing—like a domino effect, everything changed worldwide—overnight due to an unknown invader, an invisible predator, that would later be described as the Corona Virus of 2020-2021!

There seemed to be no hiding place from the disease— not even in the shelter of one's own home! With each new day, the updates compiled by the CDC and unified global organizations flooded the internet and overloaded Wi-Fi servers to disperse crucial information. In response to the unprecedented number of reported cases, the public considered Covid-19 undoubtedly terrifying and certainly a possible death-sentence if, contracted! It would be demonstrated while in the eye of the storm—many sincere and thoughtful acts of kindness and neighborly love— like the "Good Samaritan" and examples of genuine compassion. Because it was clear—we were all in this, together! The country's top analyst informed the nation that the effects of the virus were so colossally proportioned and widespread— that it ultimately had additionally created a pandemic!!

My heart pained for all of humanity: every parent, every child, every grandparent, every sibling, and every person—including the animals, on Earth and vulnerable to, and affected by this terror! Humanity deserved—a respite! One of those, "leave me be and just allow me to lie here, quietly and undisturbed," breaks or a please, show us mercy, and grant us something to help lift our hearts and brighten our days, to recall happier times," moments!! It would be on February 25, 2021: I received a call from your dad with the shocking news of your sudden death. Now nothing made sense anymore.

I had tirelessly been working on and developing a new installment to my previous book title in the hopes of reading the first printed copy to you.

I struggled for months showing no interest in and questioning myself—if I still, possessed the creative fire?

It would be seven months, on a clear, Autumn morning, that I began to reflect on the afternoon of your memorial service and what I had witnessed and learned on that sad yet incredibly beautiful day.

I recalled observing your parents bravely trying to bear up under the weight of their loss shared, but too, very private grief and surrendering to brief moments—to lean upon one another's shoulder.

A peace settled over me, as I imagined the tight friendship they'd forged in their youth before you were born, and despite decisions made that changed their courses, it seemed as if it, softly reappeared on that day to again blanket and shield them from the pain of racial divide, miscommunication—and now, this new sorrow. Thereafter they would turn and resume to offer comfort to family, including your large and beautifully diverse mix of valued friends, coworkers, and blended relationships.

It felt as if you somehow were aware—and that you did not want my last memory of you to be overshadowed by your death or the coroner's report. So, here you were encouraging me, to indiscreetly interview your community.

I do not recall how many I asked because some were standing privately to the side, and some were together in groups of 2-to5. I respectfully approached and introduced myself and proceeded to ask if they would share with me what kind of person you were?

I listened to repeated accounts paying homage to a young man beyond his years, describing you as a big-hearted, adventurous, highly creative, naturally talented, and on occasion, an outrageous daredevil, attempting bold feats and walking away with minimal injuries! As they recounted memories, tears of loss filled their eyes when reiterating as they were inevitably brought back to the present, "I wish it wasn't true because he was such a genuinely nice and fun human being, with the ability and personality to turn a funky day—into a wonderful day!"

Each reflection would then result in such a beautiful unscripted, and authentic, informal, heart-filled… eulogy, including your generous donation—formal acknowledgements made by the Life Banc organization.

On that day, there were quite a few unexpected and amazing discoveries visible in the sky and on the ground. Including your impressive network: consisting of many beautiful and vibrant colors of the true rainbow of various ages, backgrounds, degrees of education, talent, hairstyles, and authentic fashion—all unselfishly and willingly sharing a common bond; the bond of true friendship, the value of love and the hidden treasures within the presence of loss.

~ In Dedication ~

In the spirit and love that it is written, and the purpose for which it was created, I dedicate this book in (2) parts.

To all of God's beloved children.

You were created of goodness, and you are designed to be resilient. Therefore, despite the chaos and upheaval… humanity has again, prevailed, reappearing as the newer, and modern-day… Phoenix!!
Salute!

To my first-born, and forever grandson: Damien DeShaun Cramer Sharp Jr., you supersized everything, you did, e.g., loving your family and attentive of your friends, an appreciation for nature; and including those of the animal kingdom. Your pets: "Biggie" a Bully Pit that remains your rock-solid loyal… friend. In addition, to the small family of ducks you adopted and built a small private pond in your backyard for them to enjoy. You lived your life as it seems most superheroes are expected to do—accommodating the needs of others—while minimizing yours.

I didn't realize that January 11, 2022; would be our last goodbye…

That those emotional, love filled, mature and even amusing, 55 minutes shared between a grandmother and a grandson, would be the final…

I admit, and with my hand upon the Holy Book and my other hand laid over my heart, I would have insisted… our visit extend.

Your memory is etched permanently, and never to be forgotten.

My heart is hopeful that you have found your true *paradise*.
Carry on, my love… do carry on.

If you want a person to know something . . .

You tell them facts.

If you love them.

You tell them a story.

~Anonymous~

Preface

We instruct, command, and demand obedience of our domesticated pets. In some cases, enrolling them in sophisticated—obedience training and even grueling security programing courses, and all to accommodate the needs as it, relates to its owner's personal… lifestyle.

That is a tall order! Because what has been discovered in the recent years is that society has not been adhering to the very principles it expects from… "man's best friend!" News reports of horrific negligence, extreme abuse, and inexcusable acts of misconduct perpetrated upon these beautiful animals—then there is the lousy issue of owner—abandonment!

Am I capable of, responsible, suitable, or even prepared to adopt a pet?? These are the important questions that should be the first conversation— from the truth felt, in your heart.

Remember, true love does not come cheap—as it, may seem to shed fur day and night; and bellow out sounds replicating a scratched record during your REM sleep! It may tend to run around in circles leaving pattern markings on your newly installed and premium wood flooring—resembling a message to ET!!

And it might only bark when it rains or devoured half of the expensive birthday cake you just picked up from the specialty bakery—a forty-five-minute drive away for tonight's big party!

Please calm down, breathe, and try to remember that this, is a special moment—with a friend that if were necessary, would put itself between you and any—danger to protect and prove its love.

This tale is the voice and perception of the modern-day house-pet. Although filled with humor and, wit, it will surely cause one to re-think the role of the family pet!

Traditional Human and Canis Lupus Familiaris companionship is still enjoyed. However, it is evident that there is an obvious and very real demonstration of something more desired attempting expression, and even communication, or might it simply be nature's ability and objective to establish a real connection with such touching nuances—exchanged between the species?

One alpha unisex that walks upright and the other that spends its day anticipating its owner's presence after waking from a night's sleep and awaiting the morning greeting, accompanied by a spoken direct command, a hug, or a nice pat on its back?

Think about it, and in the meantime, make yourself comfortable and let's enjoy our fun Storytime together.

Chapter One

Chopper & Tank...

One chilly morning, four brothers were *dialoging* via group media communication: taking turns congratulating the youngest brother on his recent academic achievement. After several minutes of sincere, supportive comments of admirable; and mature rapport were expressed and received—it was on to the next important news of the day—the previous weekend's NFL SPORTS games with its multiple needless flimsy player fumbles and disappointing score boards!

Unaware that afar they, too, were being discussed. Not in relation to failure, but *respectively* because of love—pure puppy *love.*

The younger canine mix, although now self-assured, still *adheres* to the rules of nature and his previous training. He commences inching forward using his keen sense sniffing in one direction and then another as if following invisible and carefully laid tracks. Appearing **non-chalant** and being led only by his innocent, animal curiosity. Yet, secretly assessing the limits of the elder, territorial, more fit, and masculine breed poised stately before him unmoved, and indirectly intimidating, while apparently looking in the opposite direction!

Unable to refrain from the inclination to introduce himself and disregarding whether he would be scolded for doing so, *he deliberately began* to bark incessantly! His clever plan granted the very *response* hoped, for he now, had the attention of this lump of lean, muscle mass!

Chopper

Hello there! I didn't mean to interrupt your thoughts just wanted to introduce myself—seeing that we use to be family. My name is Chopper!

I was the proud and loyal best friend to your Uncle Vel. He was my master—and a darn good one too! Many times, when I should have been reprimanded, he would just walk away with his hands atop his head, mumbling words I am not allowed to repeat!

You know how it is being young and *impressionable.* I constantly broke from my leash when squirrels annoyed me, instigating felines taunted me, and even those grown female *canines* that would purposely prance and sashay at certain times of the month! Vel would say, "They do that because they know you like it, and to make matters worse, you put your own business out by being so hardheaded! So, when they see you chained to the tree and unable to get at 'em, then they sweat you!! ***Think about it!"***

"I wish I could trust you, "Mr. Mischievous!" Vel would continue. "But we both know what happens when I give you leash privileges. Chopper, just because you are a dog doesn't mean you toss your standards! Those dogs are not even in the same league with you! You are the man, son! You are a ***Rottweiler and Pit Bull mix, and you got heart!"***

The next time they try to use you for their personal entertainment, tell them to get themselves some real business and go bathe. Recommend that they buy a couple bars of your nana's wonderful handmade, all-natural soap, and in their case, use it with buckets of hot water!!" Vel finish

I still adore him and now realize that it is true; I use to work his nerves, especially during hectic final exams week!

We shared mutual friends, too on and off the University's campus and
my favorite fun place at the nearby doggy park!

Sometimes my master allowed me to *accompany* him to parties, and we wore the red and white or any other color in the red spectrum. He would explain that garnet and red had always been his favorite wardrobe color choices throughout his childhood and would select when he wanted to look his sharpest!

After a long back stretch and two simultaneous sneezes, then, as if on cue, the scariest sound of lethal power and gruff penetrated the entire room for ten minutes or so it seemed from oh **Mr. Show-off!**

Plus, I suspect he let off a *"quiet"* stinky too! He is so inconsiderate, behaving like I am not even here or in the same room!!

Tank

Hey, for a runt, you really got a lot to get off your chest, don't you?! I am not going to try and top your tabloid. It is a pinch melodramatic, but well, I was not a saint myself—far from it! No, sir, it did not even matter that Master D had set grand expectations due to my being an English Staffordshire, Pit Bull Terrier, and Boxer mix! Truth is that I was not interested in masquerading around as a *"gentlemen's dog."* That could be a bit risky with a name like*... "Tank!"* And would have drawn more unwanted attention and put the dawdling, dastardly crew living in my new neighborhood—on high alert!

I had already experienced a run-in with them during my first week while out minding my own business and surveying in my new backyard when the dreadful vagrants tried to TRESSPASS! DISREGARDING THE RULE THAT X MARKS THE SPOT!!

The seemingly frail one introduced himself as "**Killa** and then proceeded to list his so-called loyal and die-heart lieutenants as: **Monster, Buck Wild, Fireball, and Youngster**, and the remaining cohorts were referred to as… **Useless!**"

He referred to me as Dickey and Nigel**,** demanding that I give a-dog-a-bone! While continuing to make a few more snarky remarks such as, "Where's your pipe and butler, Mr. Nobody?!" To which I responded, "What's that barmy rubbish you speaking there, mate? I warned him, as your words are all true! I have never engaged the pipe, but **I do keep the smoke!** It is also true that I may be new around here, but I **am not brand new to the sport—Sport!"**

Nothing more than a pack of disgraceful miscreant, vagabond, underlings!!

Yes, the term **useless** is quite befitting— I found it to be most appropriate indeed!

This brings me back to my original thought…

Please understand that my rebellion was not because one day, I awoke and decided to become difficult. No, it was the actual transition itself! Transitioning from one world to another—and Master D had deviated—he did not even consult with me on the matter! This disturbed me significantly because we were boys. *"Excalibur… homies"* to the core and to the end!!

We did pretty much everything together, other than shower, and not to mention the trust factor that developed over time between us! Like you and your master, we shared friends too; some good, and some not so good, but nonetheless, they respected my master and me. I never had to become the ***"enforcer"*** because they knew it was still a set line. Although we were like an extended family, I still slept with one eye open, locked, and ready!

One evening, during an OSU game and tailgate party, Master D announced something about wedding bells and relocating…

Initially, I thought he meant me, but I, had absolutely no idea whom it could possibly be, seeing that the majority of my master's friends were male as well as their—pooches! This really put me on extreme guard, constantly patrolling and pacing, wondering if I had misunderstood his command! Had I? Or was this a form of ***new-age***

obedience training, or could it be that I had somehow mistaken my own anatomical equipment?

I retreated to my doghouse, where I secretly ***coached*** myself repetitively and reasoned with my own shadow that I sure hope these mates recall that besides being mixed breed, I am a bloody PITBULL… TOO!

Don't pretend to be audacious and have to get rectified—and dropped!

NCAA Big Game!
Ohio State University Buckeye's vs University of Michigan Wolverines

As it turned out, living in the upper "*Double O*" was not as difficult as I had imagined. However, as much as I tried, I was still unable to ignore my frequent moments of feeling melancholy, and the longing for our previous home sweet home. GO BUCKEYES!

I missed my routine veterinarian care and the gourmet food boxes containing generous treat packets given to me before leaving each visit!

Many of Master D's restaurant friends, including the store owners too, often rewarded me! The ladies would say, "***Tank,*** *you are such an impressive and handsome guy! Be careful because you could be a real heartbreaker!"*

Meanwhile, there had to be necessary *adjustments* made with a few interesting changes added that I am still scratching my head over! For instance, it was last summer, when Master D decided that I would stop breaking my leash. He referred to it, as "***running away,***" saying that if I had a mate. So, guess what? I considered fruitless—to suggest that master D, step back or take a minute and revisit the idea—to point out to him, that we might be rushing a bit here!! Breathe… Master D!

And as a reminder, permit me to redirect your attention back to the veterinarian's assessment and notes, which outlines my intellectual and potential performance development. In addition, based on both nature and science research data—that clearly states and outlines the importance of my daily playtime! Therefore, it is medically recommended! In a matter of speaking, it is vital that my youth is not interrupted—or—handled, recklessly!

Master D, I was unaware that there was such an urgency!!

Dear Reader, you must understand that once my master gets wind of a big idea—then, like a kite— he's out there!

Well… after weeks of telephoning kennels and searching through all the online licensed dog adoption network listings, within days, our luck changed. ***We received a potential… MATCH!***

Now, what I am about to share with you is not meant for your chuckles, young lad! Because I swear to you on all things good and true—this happened! And remember, I have been patient throughout this entire encounter, and we do not want the situation to become strained. Correct?

And more than anything else family first, agreed?

Very well then, I should begin with a bit of the backstory…

Tank

It was in late September, and she arrived while I was napping outside in the pleasant autumn air. Master D approached and awakened me, saying, "Hey, buddy. Guess who 's here, "with a big smile! Are you ready to meet your new friend?

How coincidental it was to me that I was dreaming of our friends before being awakened. I immediately jumped to full attention because all I recalled hearing was the term: FRIEND!

I shook my head repeatedly, appearing as if shaking an insect off my ears, but it was my genuine and nervous reaction to the utter disbelief!!

I turned to Master D, hoping our once unbreakable bond had at least a thread left; otherwise, he had some serious explaining to do!

My immediate inquiry was, are you gaming me?!

You must be trying to pull a fast one!! GOOD GRIEF, WHERE'S THE HIDDEN FLASHER! Yes, admittedly, so, and it is true, I have come to prefer urban, but this is too close to—SCI-FI!

ALL TOGETHER DIFFERENT AND NOT IN THE SLIGHTEST DOES THIS, MEET MY EXPECTATIONS, NOT A BIT!

What in blazing hell's name is it supposed to be, resembling two animals— IN ONE BREED!

A short-eared Afghan Hound in the front and an Anatolian Shepherd in the rear! It is utterly bizarre and cruel because there some things that should not be intertwined!

Yikes! Talk about being difficult to size up. It was brutal, for lack of a better word!!

I even skirted on the idea of running away… again!

I would wager that the family and friends would not refer to this, account as being just another one of *"Tank's, self-centered, attention-getting, and gallivanting shenanigans!"*

Because the difference this time would be that—I would *not return* due to my feelings of being cornered, disrespected, and BAMBOOZELED!!

NOOOO…!!!! GOOOOO AWAY!!

So, subsequently, the idea to remain caused me considerable anxiety, trepidation, acid reflux, bloating, and gout feelings in all four of my paws, too!

Really is this, a matter of take it or leave it. HUH?!?

Honestly, I wanted to be diplomatic—after all, this is my master and best friend! I also assumed Master D still understood *"**Staffordshire,**"* which is my native language, but instead of attending to my obvious pleas, he walked off to answer his *ringing side handy*. I tell you, that is such an urgent device with the most intrusive timing, isn't it?!

Chapter Two

<h1 align="center">30 days later…</h1>

Well, it turned out, for which I am grateful, that Ms. Lady is certainly no tart or thot, yet she bears an innocent and rather charming raciness that swells my chest. She liked to snuggle while watching home renovation and home-entertainment D.I.Y. shows.

We would enjoy a good romp, tussle; and "tag, it's you" racing game outside in the open backyard until one of us would tire. Then, later with permission, relax on the nice, oversized rug in the house with Master D and the family to enjoy our weekly televised, streaming family shows.

The fact that Lady was not a bore or a relentless chatterbox; and because she had not tried to finesse me, and with the pleasant ambiance— I decided to lower my guard and warm up to my new playmate.

It tickled me when observing her that she gave extra attention when the meals were completely prepared and given a striking presentation by the program's chef or culinary host. It was quite unique how Lady would behave: and as if she were hypnotized, becoming completely mesmerized by the effects of the 5G in "high-definition" cooking program!

Tank

I recall, it was a pleasant Friday mid-evening when Master D invited me to accompany him on a drive—and errand to the local fresh organic, open-air market.

Because we both had been quite busy, it occurred to me that it had been weeks since I had occupied the co-pilot seat. I really missed our private time *together.*

During the first twenty minutes of the drive, we enjoyed listening to our favorite mixed music cd tracks with a nice breeze flowing in through the half-rolled down tinted windows, like a rhythm and without need for a wordy conversation. *It was a real Rembrandt… moment!*

On the drive back home—D commented: "Hey buddy, how's everything working out with you, and your new friend? You seem to be adjusting well. Need anything?

He then reassured me of his appreciation for my cooperation and tolerance pertaining to all the recent changes. He assured me that nothing needed to change between us roadies. He reiterated that at the end of the day, his main concern was for my *wellbeing*, too.

Then he hit me with, "So **Tank,** you do understand that your friend is a **female,** right?! So, she is probably waiting for you to make the first move, huh? What do you think? Hey buddy, she is here for you!

Feeling a bit overwhelmed and already over-stimulated by Lady's charisma, without restraint, I nearly, blurted out **"STOP ALREADY MAN!"** I cannot take any more of your insensitive prying and all the unilateral decisions! How about less of the **"overseer"** and instead a bit more tact or decorum?"

"Incidentally, Master D, might I remind you, that according to the brochures you constantly show me in the patient appointment waiting area while waiting for my name to be called next, they all list *information to the local* APL and PETA! They each state that I, **Tank,** have **inalienable** rights too! But guess it slipped your mind that I can read, D!

Master D was still talking, **Tank**, are you listening to me or *Pac?!* Because it is your time, "little buddy—time for you, to be the man! So, let's run by PETCO and pick up a few nice doggy-girl treats for you to present to her. Then we will see what's really up—first base or no base! But no pressure, Ok, buddy? After this, no more surprises unless we fully discuss it first, and of course, it will be your choice as to how we handle it. Respect!

It was in that very moment, my prior and gut-wrenching *apprehension* seemed to silently fall away. Master D constantly encourages me that I am my own master, captain of my own ship, therefore not necessary to address or attach to him, the otherwise unappealing, ruthless title.

I have earnestly tried, but still find it to be my natural pedigree, and approach towards him, dutifully, as I consider him to be a fine human being, and an extraordinary chap, and leader. This is a democratic sort of command so; I will certainly work on it.

Master D and I had gallantly crossed a great divide that afternoon, and our *pact* was effectively and unanimously… renewed!

I immediately shouted, "Let's give it a go!"

The following weekend, I was putting in work throughout the day and long into the night, recessing only to go outside and find a quick dirt spot. Then it was back to my new playmate! I became so caught up that I messed around and gave her *more* of my own favorite chew toys!

She smiled and said, **"Tanky,** you're a quick learner!" I wondered: might this just be cheap … Sherpa pillow-talk? But it no longer mattered.

I was smitten and charmed by such chemistry. I *sheepishly* wagged my tail and replied, "Thank you, my darling."

It was several days later, while outside breathing in fresh air and addressing necessary personal business time, that an idea entered my thoughts. **Lady** is no slag, and she is a bit impressive— including the fact that we communicate well and do enjoy a *"jolly good"* time together!

I would certainly consider being in a committed partnership if that is what this liaison is. This is better than moonwalking, it feels great like I am on top of the world— especially when she refers to me, as her, big papa!! I couldn't refrain the impulse for a momentary… *dougie dancing!*

That's right because I, am with a capitol… B.A.D.!

LET THE GOOD TIMES ROLL!
I AM HIGH ON LIFE AND LOVE POTION: NUMBER 33!

EVERY DAY… ALL DAY!!

Just when the idea of all the fun we would continue to enjoy together, suddenly both the music and dance came to a screeching halt! It seemed like all the confetti and fireworks—abruptly stopped at the thirteenth hour on the seventh day, in mid-air!!!

As my elongated and stout, *love princess* would then announce very sternly, and from across the room—that she had a headache and then proceeded to ignore my repeated whining and groveling!

At that point, *Lady* may as well had told me to *bugger off!*

Without warning, she threw a quick and deliberate… spanner! The sudden, shocking news almost ruptured the now *deflated* family jewels!

That was in September, and it is currently the month of November, and although it might be considered as a short run, I disagree! Because it was a very profound and life-changing, *"over-the-moon and real zenith"* experience for me!

Plus, the irony of it is that **Lady** and I proved to ourselves that opposites could attract and establish an incredibly happy, medium and alliance.

In sixty days, I went from thinking and acting out as a young 1-year-old, defiant: and carefree puppy into a well-developed, *resilient, trustworthy, and mature 5-year-old, responsible adult* **canine!**

Tank and Chopper

"Chopper, make jokes if you like— but it can happen to you, as well!"

Tank warned.

"No, I agree and think it is radical! There is nothing on *Earth that compares to growing up in a caring, clean, cozy home; with human beings that welcome you!" Chopper remarked.*

Tank continued, "And much to my surprise, as of three days ago, Master D informed me that I would soon be a first-time dad! I replied, **Bravo and Eureka,** too!" I am stoked over the news because, as it turns out, mine is *a good dog life,* after-all!"

Chopper was suitably impressed, Wow… I did not expect all that from you, either Pops! He thought for a moment and then continued, "Well, I knew from the beginning that we were some of the more fortunate ones to have had great humans to care for us, and furthermore, to incorporate us into and introduce as new members of their family!"

Tank silently agreed, and after a moment, Chopper said, "Come to think of it, they made their selection from a litter that looked almost identical, and it might have been something we did that made them want us particularly. Like them pointing saying, *"Look! He's trying to touch my hand with his cute little paw through the glass! We want to adopt him; there is something extra "special" with this little one I can feel it!"* Then, you get your first ride in an automobile too!

Tank continued to listen thoughtfully. It was obvious Chopper had more to say. After another moment, Chopper didn't disappoint him, "that is why I felt so sad, for my friend, Sir Vel, when I got sick, and the veterinarian diagnosed my condition to be Parvovirus. Man, it crushed me to see Sir Vel crying real tears on my, account! I watched him race to that handsome fixture hanging on the dining room wall. Yet he continued monitoring it, as frequent as he did me for five long days! I wondered why, but I didn't bother to ask. Somehow, I understood that I was in major trouble, but this time, not with him!

Between making multiple and ***repeated*** telephone calls, including numerous online medical advice sites, campus resources, and enlisting friend's help he frantically continued to seek out additional medical and ***holistic*** treatments and every suggestion offered!"

"Needless to say: that the marathon ended, and **_time_** won by two measly … kilometers!

I miss all my uncles and cousins, and I especially miss my Nana! She smells good, she is funny and nice. Plus, she would make sure to buy the best treats for when I would come to visit, and she called me her little M&M face because of my—distinguishing brows! After his walk down memory lane, Chopper fell silent for a time, and the two enjoyed a companionable time.

"Whelp," Chopper said, "It was nice to meet you ***Tank,*** and possibly if things had gone another way, we would have gotten more acquainted as cousins and hung out. Maybe even painted the town together! You ***seem*** cool, and like you got your head on straight, so you'll be all right! Oh, and hey, congratulations on your new family too… *Dad!*

Tank responded, "Chopper, seriously, are you telling me that during this entire encounter, I have been *engaged* in a private and rather elaborate conversation with a bloody boggle? If you ask me, you have not learnt your lesson yet!

Are you resorting back to those old habits of being dodgy—again?! That is preposterous! C'mon, you do not really expect me to believe that you are *a spooky…?*

"Whoa," Tank continued that is accurate indeed— making your point!
I cannot argue with proof—since you are fading!

That is major astounding!

Chopper cut in, "Don't mean to cut you short, but I do hear the team calling me. It is my turn to play outfield catcher! There are three other members on the team that told me—they also were once selected to be companions in our family! Have you heard the name…" **Wolfie"** mentioned?

Well guess what? Uh-huh, she is there too, including the **geckos:** Bobbe, and Babe', Rosebud; and Artos, Grizzly Gray and Shar Pei, Bo Jackson and many others! It is a fun place, and we are all very much loved there!

We are happy there, too, because it is the sort of place humans say, can best be described as: splendor, and that that's what wonderful dreams are made of! Yep, that would be it!

Much to Tank's amusement, Chopper jumped up. "Ok, that's the second time I heard the umpire's whistle!

I gotta go…! Gotta run…!!

Tell everyone Chopper and all the gang said, hi! Hey Tank, Ruff… Ruff!" Tank responded, "Hopefully, this is not the last of our chats?

And in the far future when the road here closes for me if everything checks out, I will be looking you up to assume the pitcher position on your team!

A super "Cheerio" to you too, Chopper, now off you go!

Tank sat looking after his friend. What a brilliant day, he thought. I will run around the yard and chase those meddling Black-crows—nonsense, I meant, those greedy, annoying tick couriers, bushytailed squirrels including their willfully stubborn, *co-conspirators*, and noisy blue jays to which I find both to be a contradiction of the term… *beauty!*

Tonight, when Master D inquire how I spent my day? I'll answer, with family!" Umm… I wonder what Master D will think of my conversation with *Chopper*? Won't he be surprised? Ha-ha…!

Fancy that, what an eventful day indeed!!

Whistling …

"Love Is the Key" … Maze featuring Frankie Beverly

Yeah… baby-baby!

Brightest Cheers to all!

BONUS FEATURE!

Adventures in Tom-Land, USA

Is it fact or merely *antiquated* fiction of the possibility that animals, particularly with domesticated cats, and dogs—do understand more than just our hand and body language or gestures? And in fact, can *interpret* the basic verbalized human language? Well, after personally witnessing firsthand our own pets, I know they can.

In addition, to accounts expressed by other proud pet owners excited to share this remarkable discovery with anyone who might listen. Then there's the amusing recorded home videos submitted to television shows from contestants hoping theirs is selected to be viewed by audiences around the world and voted the most unique pet performance and win the grand prize!

In conclusion, it is profoundly evident when demonstrated by the professional dog trainer or handler, during a training session—with the trainee as it again, supports the facts and provides the proof.

Therefore, I will allow this short story to illustrate. Enjoy!

INTRODUCING…

Now without further ado, please welcome our special guest, Tom and on occasion known as… Tomcat!

It was the close of the school year and the start of summer vacation. My older sister invited me to come spend the summer at her home in Los Angeles, California and said, Tom would be permitted to join me!

She had planned a fun trip to Disneyland Park Resort and a Hollywood tour! I described the itinerary in each exciting detail to Tom so, he would not become anxious by all the new stimuli, due the length of the trip, unfamiliar sounds, and his limited freedom to roam.

Ideally, I thought what a wonderful vacation it would be for Tom and me!

Tom surprised us, how well he settled in and quietly adapted to the new surroundings. Including his new daily activity of relaxing and soaking up some West Coast sunshine and California dreaming—while listening to the hip melodies that flowed from the 1970's R&B… into his pointy ears!

Around the age of 13 or 14 years old, my father brought home a kitten as *a gift* to my mother—and said he preferred the name: Tom. It was a male kitten. His fur was a jet-black color, soft and shiny. He had a long stripe or snow-white underbody—like *a tuxedo shirt* and the same color on the tips of his front paws. He quickly adapted and grew with his new family.

My mother would decide to rename him… **"Bullet"** she said that the name best suited him because of his *amazing and daring agility!* He could dart, jump, and run so fast inside and outside of our house!

Oftentimes, causing those observing dizziness! Plus, he had intelligence just as swift because he clearly accepted his *new given name* and, quite possibly identified with it!!

Bullet's funniest trick to me—occurred when he would return after a full day of roaming about the neighborhood (a common trait of a *tomcat…* I'm told) and using his front paws to—*knock on the door for entry!* And without fail he would make a bee line—for the kitchen! We could hear him purring—his purrs mimicked that of a *serenade—as a*n attempt to persuade my mother for food while she was in the kitchen cooking.

He knew the rules—the kitchen was ALWAYS OFF LIMITS—TO HIM! Occasionally he could be a naughty rebel—slip by the guard and through the perimeter! Aware of this behavior; and without hesitation or forgiveness on the menu—my mother sternly scolded **Bullet** to move out of her way and go eat his own (emphasize on: **Tomcat**!!) food in the breezeway next to the basement door!

Yet each time she walked by him—he would lift his paw towards her as if requesting pity to permit him the honor of a sampling *taste-test* from the deliciously aromatic (substance ***in the big yellow glass bowl***), and the steaming pots containing the meal being prepared for the family!!

He all but *yelled "For the love of God…please, Madam, have you no mercy for your—Bullet?!"*

It was also, interesting to me that despite there being five roomy bedrooms in our house, but that ***Bullet*** chose to sleep at the foot of (my) bed every night; and remained consistent with his slumber choice—even when I slept away at a relative's home for the weekend! As it goes to say, he and I amicably did develop *a mutual bond* —we appreciated similar taste in *junk food, music,* and respected each other's need for personal space, as well.

Bullet far exceeded the falsehood and superstition given by *old wives-tales and folklores...* warning that ***"they're evil and not safe to fall asleep around because a cat would steal your breath away!"***

He certainly displayed *a mysterious side and slightly* moody, but non-threatening. Typically, the trait most resembling such behavior exhibited during his outside *fieldwork* or when investigating— crotched low (like his safari, big cat cousins) to sneak up on prey or my no. 2 yellow pencil, when I was working on a homework assignment. ***Bullet*** must have mistaken the yellow linear object whirling and circling about as if somehow moving on its own and that disturbed him!

Bullet was not very fond of *Mother Nature's* uneventful— seasonal lightning strikes, jarring thunderclaps nor the explosive ***Ka-boom*** sounds from the traditional (*beautiful and festive*), **July 4th,** Summertime fireworks!

Bullet's distress would be compounded by emergency vehicles with bright red flashing lights—and loud sirens so, as a result or may in his retaliation— he would make every (annoying) moaning sound *to express*—his absolute contempt for them all!!

Another unusual *trait* I noticed about **Bullet** was that when you spoke directly to him—he would turn to look at whom it was speaking to him, and thereby respond based on—his findings! And if you asked him a question—he appeared to respond according to whether it was a statement, a command or a… question!

In addition, to the multitude of battles Bullet had won over the years defeating his enemies be they of the air; or *brazenly* hidden in a tree, as well as the ones that walked upon the ground—it did not matter if they were BIG or small; his skills and *reputation* never waned! I recall a most hilarious, but true to life moment—it was the time I had witnessed, Bullet standing up on his back legs in a boxing pose!!

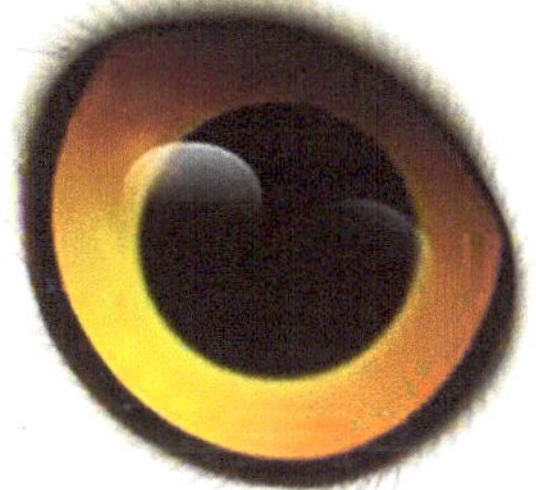

His claws were protruding like ***pearl hooked-daggers*** with an equally precise; and stalwart reach permitting him to strike his opponent—squarely in its hazel-green colored optics!

Impressed yet realizing that recently I had seen a similar display on *a local* **Cleveland, Ohio** television interview premiering the history making and undisputed, *(**THREE TIME** …**heavy weight legend**) **and my daddy's second favorite boxer in the entire world***.

…Mr. Muhammad Ali!!!

The big sports networks were all reporting that it would be a live telecast from Manila… ***"THE THRILLA, IN MANILA"*** in the Philippines!! And it offered a boxing ring epic announcement of the ***winner take all bouts!!!*** Because another knockout had been— predicted!

Bullet must have heard the announcement too and decided on the exact outcome for his bout—as well! He was a *tuxedo* wearing **"cool cat"** and still reigning, neighborhood… unprecedented **champion!!**

58

So, as you can now *imagine*—I was quite **entertained** by our pet cat and felt incredibly sad when he eventually moved on—due to age and failing health. My family had welcomed several pets—during my childhood and lovingly mentioned each—from time to time. However, **Bullet** was by far my favorite pet with his rosy, pink nose, *razor* sharp teeth, whiskers, and all.

There are special friendships formed that can last a lifetime.

Acknowledgements

To my grandchildren, thank you for your un-conditional love and for valuing both my wisdom and humor—for referring to me as the best grandmother that ever lived!! Although that is unlikely, I certainly appreciate the thought.

To my children: (*my very own beautiful womb seeds*), an extra special *thank you* for your love, respect; and for always believing in me, and for being a constant support of my lifestyle and work. *To all my family and extended, thank you* for your everyday love and enjoyable kindred.

I appreciate and am grateful to each of you for recognizing my authenticity and joining in the grand celebration by acknowledging *your very own shinning gifts—within you, too!*

I would also like to express my *humble and heartfelt gratitude* for the individual effort put forth by three incredibly talented people that helped me to *translate what I imagined into the visible. Thank you* for your professional services, and for genuinely and equally regarding both the characters and the incredible, finished results! ***Muniba Khan,*** animation scene, and page designer, extraordinaire! ***Marsha Fulton,*** proofreading and editing services, "eagle-eyes!" and ***Brian D Sharp,*** Brian Sharp Studios LLC, for your continued generosity, knowledge, and brilliant technology skills!!

Because *LOVE* really does make all things better—as the world goes around and around.

~Warmest Gratitude ~

From the Author

Dear readers,

I am not a celebrity, nor a powerful politician, or a well-noted pioneer physicist (which are all important and amazing!). Therefore, this unfamiliarity makes me, more, or less, a stranger to you. So, I decided to ask key people that I, regard as pretty "special" and because they bear great principle and integrity to do me the honor of sharing a short and personal commentary.

They agreed.

Thank you.

Commentaries

Denise Sharp, a person I have known for over twenty years, is worthy of literary merit, a quality shared by all works of fiction with aesthetic value and flare. Although the concept of literary merit has been criticized as being subjective, Denise's love for writing, particularly poetry, reflects her giving personality, religious foundation, and human spirit manifested in her life and in her works. Over the years, she has displayed skills for parenting, maintaining family relationships, nurturing friendships, and for writing poetry. When she walks into a room, you will know she is there, so enjoy the view, the essence of her being and her words.

—Phyllis M. Thomas, M. Ed., Retired Professor of Education

"I have known Denise Sharp personally and professionally, for ten years. She has always had interest in writing compelling content. In the years I have known her, she has demonstrated exceptional skill and competence. I have always been amazed by her passion for creating high-quality written content that would appeal to many audiences. In addition, Denise has an excellent rapport with everyone. She is enthusiastic, humble, and honest. She has excellent communication skills, which helps her connect with people of all ages. Whenever there is an occasion at home, Denise is always called upon to speak because she is naturally articulate."

—Grovine Buffington, M.Ed

It is my honor and privilege to speak on behalf of the artistic and creative development of Denise Sharp. As a member of her community, as knowing her as well as I do over the last 5 years, I am glad to say that she is indeed an author… extraordinaire. Her life views, opinions; and outlook are beyond measure. Not only does she write with great character and integrity, but also stands as a shining example of what African American Queens ought to be!

Dr. Greg Gissentaner
Senior Bishop & Presiding Overseer

Kingdom Life Church

Starting the list is our white feathered, **red crowned, farm-raised, chicken**—now please keep in mind that initially, Charlie was introduced to us as our new… pet. However, by the third or fourth month of living in our home and well cared for and **generously feed--** including fun entertainment. In addition, living in a very sturdy, customized wooden coop—designed and built by our mother for the comfort, safety, and a means of monitoring **Charlie's** activities; and to better manage the daily flying of loose, airy— feathers! Well…, **Charlie,** it was fun while… it lasted!

Onyx colored **(German-Shepherd mix…)** the pointy-eared, over-zealous and protective, fried egg eating, brassier stealing—incessantly sniffing shoes and under the front door! A constant nemesis—disrupting the monthly meter readings required from PUCO—chasing away the gas man and, the daily mail carriers—always a security guard… **Mr. Midnight!!**

Next up: An **(Irish Setter/Cocker Spaniel mix.)** A combination of which every girl envisions for herself—and this one indeed had them both: beauty and brains! A sure finalist for covers in: Modern Dog and American Kennel Club, magazines! Intelligence, poise, beauty, great teeth and obedient!! Yes, that was the very gorgeous… **Snoopy!**

2) Ebony colored and (1) Ivory colored **(French/Toy Poodles);** defiant… **Pierre!** Temperamental: **Peppe'** (every time I would visit my big-sister, **Pepe'** whimpered at the sight of my infant son's baby bottle filled with baby formula—until we realized and gave him one as too!

New to the block yet maintained her naturally sophisticated posture—and took names later was none other than the charcoal gray colored, Siamese, feline … **Ms. Bambi!** Along with her cheese popcorn, peanut butter cookie eating; and dancing machine—displaying phenomenal, aerobatic agility in mid-air from the top of the stair banisters, and landing precisely at the feet of unsuspecting visiting, guests!! **Bambi's** tag team accomplice and cat cousin … **Fluffy!**

Without further delay, the shy and adorable girl with her very own wardrobe (in the 1970's!!) including a baby-doll and a fancy teddy bear collection… was the little **Ms. Gee**

Proudly, hailing from Cincinnati, Ohio; and home of the … Reds, a baseball team that once dominated the National League's/ World Series title during the 1970's—alongside one of the youngest franchises ever to reach the NFL playoffs 1988!! That's right—that would be quarterback: Boomer Esiason: AFC Championship—the team: Cincinnati Bengals!!! His hometown—close to the Riverfront Stadium is none other than our: larger than life, yet, obedient, playful; and remarkably agile, a pooch with both charm and memory… recall!! **(Old English/Shaggy, Sheep Dog)** Yours truly… **Alfie!!!**

1 pair of **Parakeets:** bearing shades of tropical green, yellow, and white feathers… I named them after the popular characters: Luke Skywalker and Princess Leia (from George Lucas', 1977 hit movie: Star Wars).

Nearing the finish line—was my last and (third) **Parakeet** (the cleverly courageous, chirping while bowing up; and down to the beat—when we played our Classic R&B albums on the stereo… the infamous "Breakout King" … **Mr. Blu!!**

It was on a lovely Sunday afternoon on: Mother's Day (1986). After having his cage thoroughly refreshed—the door of the birdcage had accidently been left ajar; and **Mr. Blu** would decide on that day to—reclaim his freedom! He sat on the porch banister for hours—flapping his wings and disregarding our coaxing as we repeatedly pleaded for him to return—before climbing to the roof to rest and focus—after several hours sitting there… Blu flew away.

2 more **(German Shepherds):** Welcome, the neighborhood terror and rebel rouser, with a standing height to that of an average, man—it is the WILD and outrageous…**Duke!), and Count D'Marco!**

Although, it was a tearful departure (1991), please give a salute to the young, suburbanite and newly graduated, **Officer Dominique!!** Fortunately, he was adopted out—and miraculously landed into a Special Forces-Canine, Police Program!!! Interestingly, it turned out to be a happy conclusion after all☺

My sister's pooch: **(Wolf/Collie mix.)** the one and only helpful, protective; and uncannily wise, attentive, lovable, and caring… was our watchful mama… Wolfe aka: Wolfie!

(Pitt Bull): Inquisitive, affectionate, obedient, LOYAL, and tidy—with human-like chiseled… cheekbones; and Ice-blue, topaz colored—eyes!! The fierce yet mothering; sweetheart, and the real "lady of the house …" our girl… **Angel!**

1 **(Red-Stripe Turtle): Rainbow**, my daughter's— (another of those I, promise…') and had to have birthday presents!!

2 **(Bichon Frise's**.): 1 residing on the West Coast and 1 residing on the East Coast) Our sister living in L.A. swooned over the lovely, and adorable surprise birthday gift from her husband— she affectionately named: **Rosebud.**

Stand back and make room for the big, little man that rules with an iron fist! He takes his job very seriously and considers his owner and human brother as real a family—as family could be and their trusted reliance upon his bravery and strength! And rightfully so, his name is: **King!**

1 **(German Weimaraner)** Oh such a devoted best friend! He so loved his owner! Oftentimes, when his owner was away on a long 36-hour medical work shift, **Artos** could become moody because he only recognized his owner—as the Alpha! However, because he understood his owner's connection with family—he meticulously and eventually embraced you. I considered it, both hilarious and quite impressive to observe him, when given instruction or a command from his Opa or Oma and other family members—as he fully understood the German language! Tall with beautiful, hypnotic-like eyes and a muscled, long frame; warmly tolerant and forgiving of his English-speaking family members visiting from America. Thank you, **Artos!**

3 **(Yorkshire Terrier)** Described as affectionate with big personalities, and in this case that is three times the love! Fitted in pint size, tailored, glam style, attire with a dash of flair making each ready for the runway at a moment's click! Meet Dad: **Ponchie, his son Grizzly. and Marie.** Marie would be adopted into the family

2 years later and after establishing boundaries and designated roles they now live happily together—teamwork and doting over their owner!

2 (Leopard Geckos): Bobbe' and Babe' joined our family against my better judgment. It was on my son's thirteenth birthday and despite my answer being—no way, ABSOLUTELY NOT in this house, and they are somewhat "snaky" looking too!!!

With tears streaming, bartering for additional chores; and promising to make the honor roll repeatedly—he managed to convince me into purchasing as his birthday gift! Including the guarantee that this, was the only gift he wanted—no new video games, Jordan's, or any of the latest…! Just a gecko!! He assured me that he had already done the research to familiarize himself; and he felt quite confident to care for one and would continue to learn more—given the lizards 10–15-year lifespan!!

After a few years of reminding him per our agreement eventually they (2 because store clerk advised—buy another as mate at the same time—or first gecko may reject when try to introduce and harm the new one!)

Bobbe and Babe' were placed in my care when my son graduated, and as a new first-year student left home for college.

So, I renewed our Petco membership; and as they continued to happily grow—to my surprise, I genuinely developed a fondness of the cute, little lizards.

A variety of freshwater and tropical fish rounded up the daily family fun!

Each with its own **one-of-a-kind** personality, and remarkable aptitude…unanimously are being recognized for a stellar performance, individually and as a group! Congratulations!!!

And the audience goes wild!!!

Author's Biography

Denise Sharp is a natural creative at heart and a loving soul. She is an enthusiastic and accomplished poet, writer, storyteller, artist, and independent small business owner. As a writer her gift with words allows for the reader to travel with her and walk the roads she has walked as a seeker in the quest of Divine, Truth and Self-discovery. These traits are evident and experienced in the healing, Reiki infused, gemstone jewelry designed by her for clients. Her greatest joy she admits, is being a mother. In addition, to the double crown bestowed her as a grandmother! This all makes for a full life, and why she cherishes family fun gatherings and memorable celebratory events because she considers her family to be a gift, inspiration, and her grand reward. Modupe' Amin.

Other books by the author:

To Travel Lite, Part 1

Upcoming…

The Classic Edition

To Travel Lite, Part 1 and 2

TO TRAVEL LITE, Part 1.5: The Day Two Canines Informally Confessed.
Written, Cover Design, Characters, Interior Design, Promotional Video and Voice-over.
Created by Denise Sharp.

THAT'S ALL FOLKS!

Adobe Stock License Image ID Number: 264289119
Adobe Stock License Image ID Number: 42197549
<a href="https://www.vecteezy.com/free-vector/
sunflower">Sunflower Vectors by Vecteezy</a>

https://library.biblioboard.com/content/f74a8486-9af8-4494-b4b1-
b4a010f13123 (original draft previewed 2017)

With paid Primary Subscription and in rightful compliance for
commercial, media, web, and personal use the illustrations in To
Travel Lite, Part 1.5, The Day Two Canines Informally Confessed,
with *__Bonus Feature:__ Adventures in Tom Land, were sourced @
Freepik.com. In addition, the use of **Freepik Company, Free Fonts/
Typography** are herein respectfully mentioned in accordance with the
Freepik [Attribution] and license agreement.

Microsoft/Word and Grammarly Editing Software for professional
writers and business documents.

The Left and Right Style Maniacs LLC
www.theleftandrightstylemaniacs.net

FRIENDS
are
like
STARS
you don't
always
SEE THEM
but
you allways know
THEY ARE THERE...